A Chimp in the Family

By Charlotte Becker

Illustrated by Seymour Fleishman

A TAB BOOK

Published and distributed by TAB Books, Inc., an affiliate of
Scholastic Magazines. 33 West 42nd Street, New York 36, N. Y.

Copyright 1953 by Julian Messner, Inc. Special contents copyright 1957 by TAB Books, Inc. This TAB edition is published by arrangement with Julian Messner, Inc. Published 1957 by TAB Books, Inc. Third printing, August, 1959

Mr. Davis was walking up and down his pet store with a baby chimpanzee in his arms. He was trying to figure out what to do with the little ape.

That morning a sailor had sold Maggie to him. She came from the warm forests of faraway Africa. Sooner or later a circus or a zoo or someone who liked unusual pets would buy Maggie. But, until then, the store was no place for her.

Mr. Davis looked at the row of cages in his shop. There were big and little ones, but none big enough for Maggie. Besides, Maggie had never lived in a cage.

Mr. Davis looked at his chimpanzee and asked, "Why did I ever buy you, anyway?"

"Because you're a dope, a dope, a dope!" screamed a big red parrot.

Maggie was scared — so scared that she grabbed Mr. Davis by the collar. To quiet her, he sat down at his desk and stroked her fur.

Maggie put her head on his shoulder and then gave him a sweet smile. She must like me, thought Mr. Davis.

It seemed that Maggie liked his desk, too. She playfully reached for a drawer and opened it. Inside there was a neat stack of letters. Maggie pulled out the whole stack.

"No, no!" scolded Mr. Davis.

So Maggie dropped the letters—every single one of them, all over the floor.

"What if you open my snake cages!" cried Mr. Davis.

Just then the telephone rang. It was Mrs. Davis, and she asked, "When will you come home?"

"I don't know yet — I may be late, dear,"

answered Mr. Davis. He looked at Maggie, and suddenly he knew just what to do with her. "Tell the children I have a surprise for them," he said.

It was snowing outside, so Mr. Davis bundled Maggie into a heavy blanket. He took her to his car. Off they went all the way uptown to the big apartment house where the Davis family lived.

Peg and Tom were waiting for him. When the

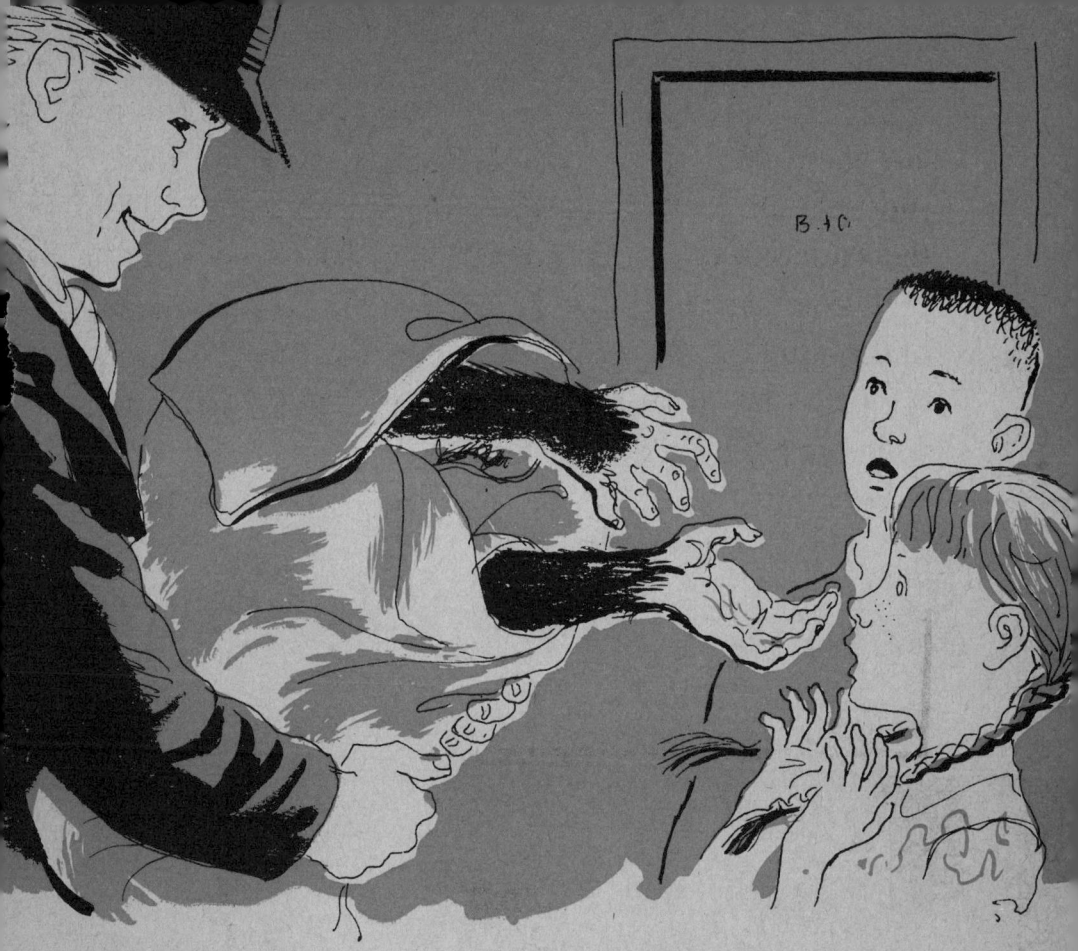

doorbell rang, they ran down the hall.

Peg saw the big blanket and clapped her hands. "Oh, a baby!" she cried. But as she reached for the baby, two long furry arms shot out toward her. "Ohhhh!" shrieked Peg.

The arms went around Father's neck, and Maggie clung to him. "It's a baby all right," said Father. "But a baby chimp."

"WHAT?" called Mother, coming down the hall. "A chimp? A *chimpanzee* chimp? Oh, no!"

"Oh, yes, dear," answered Father.

He carried Maggie into the living room and sat her down on the couch. At first the chimpanzee didn't know what to do. She just stared at the children and they stared at her.

"Come on, be nice to Maggie," said Father. "She likes to be petted."

But when Tom touched Maggie, she drew back her lips and bared her teeth. "Uh, uh, uh," she barked.

"Don't be afraid," said Father. "Maggie will be all right after she gets to know you. And you will have plenty of time to become friends, for Maggie is going to live with us for a while."

"Is this a joke?" asked Mother. "How can we keep a chimp in a city apartment? What will the landlord say? What will the neighbors say? Why, the lady upstairs will have a fit! You know how everything upsets her."

"Well, I can't keep her in the store," said Father.

"Then sell her right away." Mother was getting angry. "I want you to know I will *not* be a baby-sitter for a chimp."

Maggie looked as if she were ready to cry.

Peg petted her, and this time Maggie liked it.

"Oh, Mother," said Peg, "I'll sit for Maggie. Taking care of her will be more fun than playing with dolls."

"I'll take care of her, too," said Tom.

Mrs. Davis looked at Maggie. "But what will we do with her? Every last child on the block will be in here to play with her, and I won't have that. And the lady upstairs will complain about the noise."

Tom laughed. "Oh, no. Every last child won't be here. Half of them have the mumps."

Father jumped up excitedly. "*Mumps!* Why, Maggie may catch them. She can get nearly every disease people get. And I don't know what we'll do with her if she gets the mumps."

"See," said Mother. "We can't keep her here."

Father didn't give in. "We *must* keep her here! But we will make a strict rule—no one is to know that Maggie lives with us."

Mother sighed and went into the kitchen to get supper ready.

Then Tom and Peg went down into the storeroom

of the apartment house to look for their old baby things. They soon found what they needed—a crib and a high chair.

The crib went into Peg's room. "Maggie can sleep here and I'll look after her," said Peg.

The high chair went into the kitchen. Father put Maggie in it and fed her Pablum from a big blue bowl. She seemed to like the Pablum, for she ate one spoonful after the other.

"What else does she eat?" asked Tom.

"Milk, bananas, orange juice, and just about everything that a human baby does," replied Father. Then he added, "She eats nicely. And she has good table manners, too."

"I think I can teach her to feed herself," said Peg.

She put a spoon in Maggie's hand and led it to the bowl, then into Maggie's mouth. But when Peg gave the spoon to the little ape, Maggie behaved the way human babies sometimes do. She threw the spoon down on the floor. Then she snatched the bowl and gobbled the Pablum straight from the dish.

"This will never do!" cried Peg, pulling the bowl away.

As Peg bent down to pick up the spoon, the chimp's hands shot out for the bowl. Quick as a

flash, Maggie turned it upside down. Plop! Down went the bowl—right over her head. What a mess!

Maggie shrieked with laughter and beat on her high chair with her fists.

Tom and Peg giggled. But Mother said in a nasty-nice voice, "Did someone tell me she has good table manners?"

Tom pulled the bowl off Maggie's head while

Peg ran to the sink to get a dishcloth.

"I think Maggie is tired," said Father. "She has had enough excitement for one day."

After Peg washed the Pablum out of Maggie's hair, everyone helped the chimp get ready for bed.

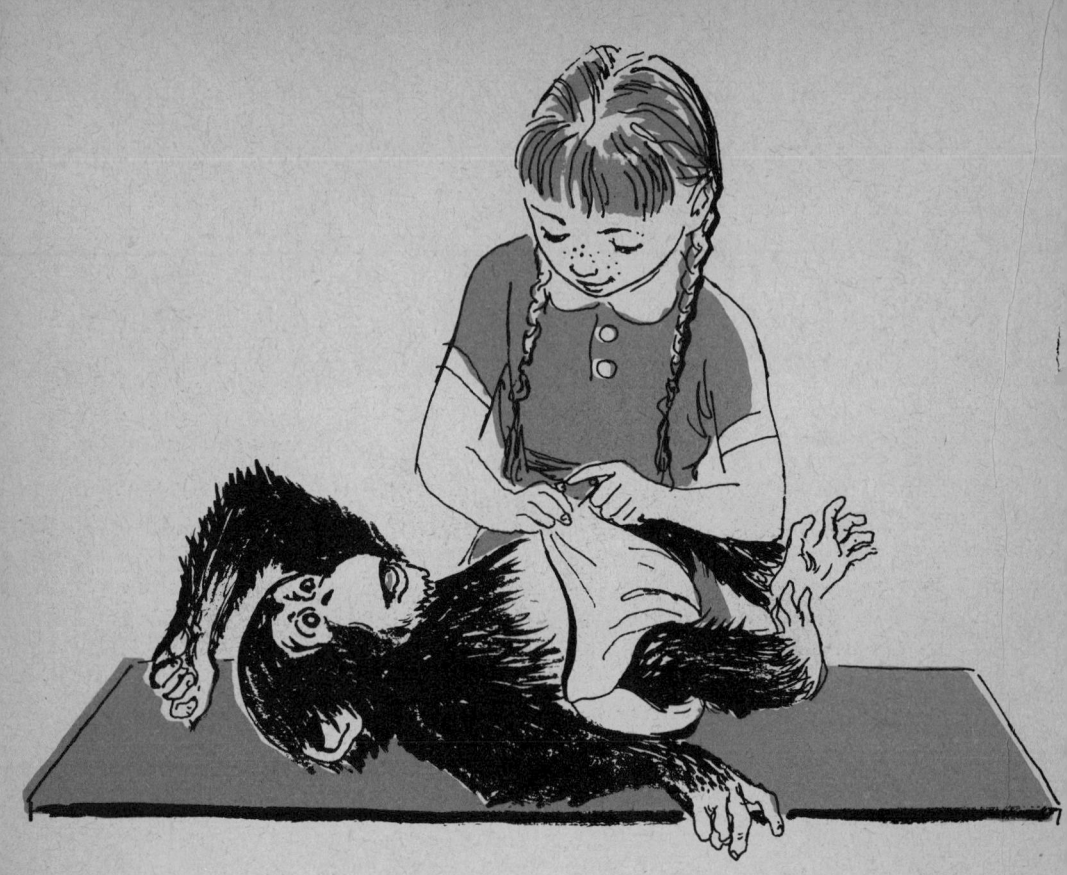

"Will she need diapers?" asked Peg.

"Plenty of them," said Father. "Perhaps later on we can train her to go to the bathroom. But use some old pieces of cloth for tonight."

Mother found some towels that she had thrown into the ragbag. Peg folded them to make a diaper while Maggie watched. Then the little ape lay quietly on the bedroom table and let Peg pin up her diaper.

16

Tom decided Maggie needed pants, too. He brought out an old pair of striped swimming trunks from his room and put them on the chimpanzee.

Maggie looked so funny in her striped pants that the children began to laugh. But Maggie wanted to cry. Her feelings were hurt.

Father talked to her in a soothing voice. Then he led Maggie to a long mirror to show her how nice she looked.

Maggie's face broke into a happy smile. She dashed up to the mirror to talk to the other chimpanzee. She even tried to reach around the mirror to find that other little ape. But when she felt the cold glass, she quickly backed away.

As soon as the crib was ready, Maggie climbed up one side and jumped right in. She crawled under the covers and lay on her back with her arms over her head. She was really tired.

Peg tucked in the covers. "I know what you need, Maggie—a doll—a chimp doll—all your own. But tonight I'll let you have my Nicki."

Peg picked up her old rag doll and held it in front of Maggie. Maggie snatched Nicki and hugged her.

After closing the bedroom door, Peg stood outside

"It usually dies, since wild animals don't take medicines. In the zoo, things are different. Those that get sick are treated by special animal doctors called vets."

"Don't worry about Maggie, Father," said Peg. "We'll see that she doesn't get sick. We won't need a vet for her."

"The main thing to remember is that her body

is almost like yours. She needs to follow the same health rules you do, now that she lives in the city."

"And that reminds me," said Mother. "Growing children need plenty of sleep. To bed—both of you!"

Early the next morning, before the sun was up, Maggie stirred in her crib. The windows were open and the room was chilly. The heat was not on yet. Maggie pushed aside her covers and climbed out of the crib.

Peg was still asleep.

Maggie shivered a little, but the cold didn't bother her much. She walked quietly around the room and studied her new home. She opened all the drawers in the chest and pulled *everything* out of them. Then she threw Peg's socks and underthings here, there, and everywhere.

When there was nothing else left in the chest, Maggie looked in the closet. The clothes on the hangers frightened her. Maybe she thought people were hiding in them. Anyway, she shut the closet door.

Maggie looked around for something else to do.

In the corner of the room she saw a long pipe that went from the floor to the ceiling. When the

heat was on, the pipe carried steam to the floors above.

Maggie dashed to the pipe. Up she climbed, until she reached the ceiling. There she found a little space around the pipe. It had been built that way because the metal of the pipe becomes a little bigger whenever it is heated. Of course, Maggie didn't know this.

She was very curious about the space around that pipe. So she poked one of her long, hairy hands up through the hole.

Suddenly there was a shriek from the apartment

upstairs. Then came more shrieks and footsteps and excited voices out in the hall.

The Davis doorbell rang and rang. Father jumped out of bed, put on his robe, and ran to the door.

Peg and Tom followed him. So did Mother.

The lady from upstairs was standing outside, waving her hands wildly. The apartment superintendent was trying to quiet her.

"A long, hairy hand is coming out of my floor!" yelled the lady. "This house is haunted. It's a loose hand. Oh, Mr. Davis, be careful!"

The superintendent looked at her as if she were crazy. "How can a hairy hand get through your floor?" he asked. "You were dreaming. I'm sure you were dreaming."

"Mag—er——" said Peg. But she quickly stopped herself. "*Maybe*, I mean. Maybe it was a dream."

Father smiled at the lady in a kindly way. "I'm sorry you are upset," he said. "Please take another look. I think you will find that everything is all right."

As soon as the door closed, Peg ran into her room. Father and Mother and Tom dashed after her. When Maggie saw them, she scampered down the pipe and jumped into the crib. Then she hid under the covers.

"I told you so," said Mother. "We just can't keep an ape in a city apartment."

Later, when the heat was on, Peg and Tom led Maggie into the bathroom. Father had bought her a bright red face cloth and a toothbrush with a bright red handle.

Tom showed Maggie how to unscrew the cap of the toothpaste. Her fingers were nimble, and she learned this very quickly.

Next Tom showed Maggie how to put the paste on her toothbrush. He helped her move the brush up and down and around her teeth and gums. Maggie liked doing this and soon she was brushing her teeth for all she was worth.

Father stopped in to watch. He laughed. "Maggie, if you brush your teeth like that every morning and night, and if you eat the right foods, you'll never

have any bad teeth. Same to you, dear children."

As Tom and Peg started brushing their teeth, Father left.

Maggie liked the taste of the toothpaste so much that she decided to eat it straight out of the tube. She picked up the tube and squeezed and squeezed it.

"No, no!" yelled Tom, grabbing the toothpaste.

Then Peg tried to wash Maggie's face. But she kept pushing away the bright red cloth.

"Gee," said Peg, "I wonder how mother chimps wash their babies."

"They lick them, I think."

"Well, I'm not going to do that! Tom, let me wash you to show Maggie what I'm trying to do."

Tom giggled and made funny faces while he held out one hand, then the other. His sister washed and dried them, while Maggie watched every move that Tom made.

Then she copied him. She even tried to make the same kind of funny faces that he did. But after her hands were washed and dried, she surprised the children. She held out one foot, then the other!

"She's a smart little chimp, all right," said Tom. "After all, her feet are almost like her hands."

Since it was Saturday morning, Tom was eager to go outside to play. But Peg said, "I'd rather stay with Maggie."

Peg decided to take a bath. As she turned on the water, Maggie watched with great interest. After Peg was in the tub, Maggie splashed the water around a little. But she didn't want to take a bath.

Maggie had another idea. She went to the sink and turned on the water there. Peg was so busy washing herself that she didn't see the sink fill up.

Higher and higher went the water. And then it overflowed. Maggie stood under the sink and let the water pour down on her. She had her own little shower.

"You imp of a chimp!" yelled Peg, jumping out of the tub. She wrapped herself in a big towel, and then put a little towel around Maggie. "You'll catch a cold for sure! Oh, Mother! M-O-T-H-E-R!"

When Mrs. Davis saw the bathroom floor, she groaned. "Hurry and mop it, Peg. Hurry, before the lady downstairs comes to complain about water dripping through her ceiling." Then she scolded Maggie. "Now don't you ever do that again!"

The weather was very cold, and Tom soon came back into the house. He spent the rest of the day indoors with Peg and Maggie.

Maggie played like a little child. She built with blocks. She scribbled with crayons, and she pulled

a little wagon all over the house. She dragged Nicki around with her until Father came home with a chimp doll for her. Then the little ape dropped Nicki and cuddled her new doll.

"I wonder if she knows it looks like her," said Peg.

Peg and Tom had to watch Maggie every minute to keep her out of mischief. Only one thing went wrong. That happened when Maggie spied a bowl of bananas. She grabbed a banana and peeled it.

Tom and Peg had so much fun watching Maggie eat the banana they forgot to pick up the peel.

Of course it was Mother who slipped on the peel! And of course Mother didn't like that *one bit*.

By the time evening came, Maggie was worn out. Father noticed a funny look in her eyes. "I

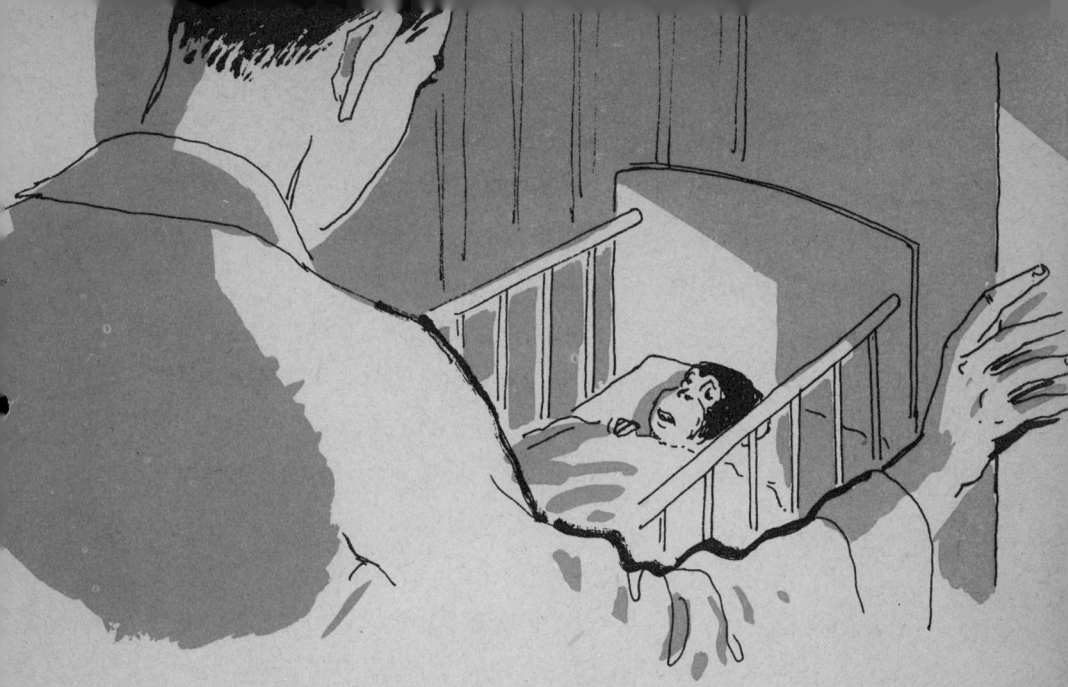

sure hope she's not catching a cold," he said. "Let's get her into bed fast."

That night, after the children were asleep, Mr. Davis heard a cough, then another cough. He tiptoed into Peg's room. Sure enough, it was Maggie who was coughing.

Father decided to take no chances. He carried sleeping Peg into his room and put her into his own bed. Then he woke Maggie and gave her an aspirin that had been mixed with some mashed-up banana.

Maggie's eyes were watery and her head felt feverish. "Kerchoo, kerchoo," she sneezed.

She had one coughing spell after another. In

between them Maggie sobbed, "Ooh, ooh, ooh."

Father ran to the phone to call the animal doctor who looked after the dogs, cats, snakes, and parrots in the pet store. But the vet didn't answer.

Father decided, then, to call Dr. Sampson, who was the children's doctor. He was in, and Mr. Davis quickly told him about Maggie and her cough.

"But I've never worked with chimps before," said Dr. Sampson.

Mr. Davis pleaded with him to come.

Finally Dr. Sampson said, "Well, maybe I can handle Maggie. Scientists test new medicines on apes because they are so much like people. I think I can treat her just like a human baby." Then he added, "But please, Mr. Davis, keep my visit a secret. I can't afford to have people call me an ape doctor!"

When Dr. Sampson saw how sick Maggie was, he said, "I'm glad I came. We can't have the children catch this. Maggie has a *very* bad case of

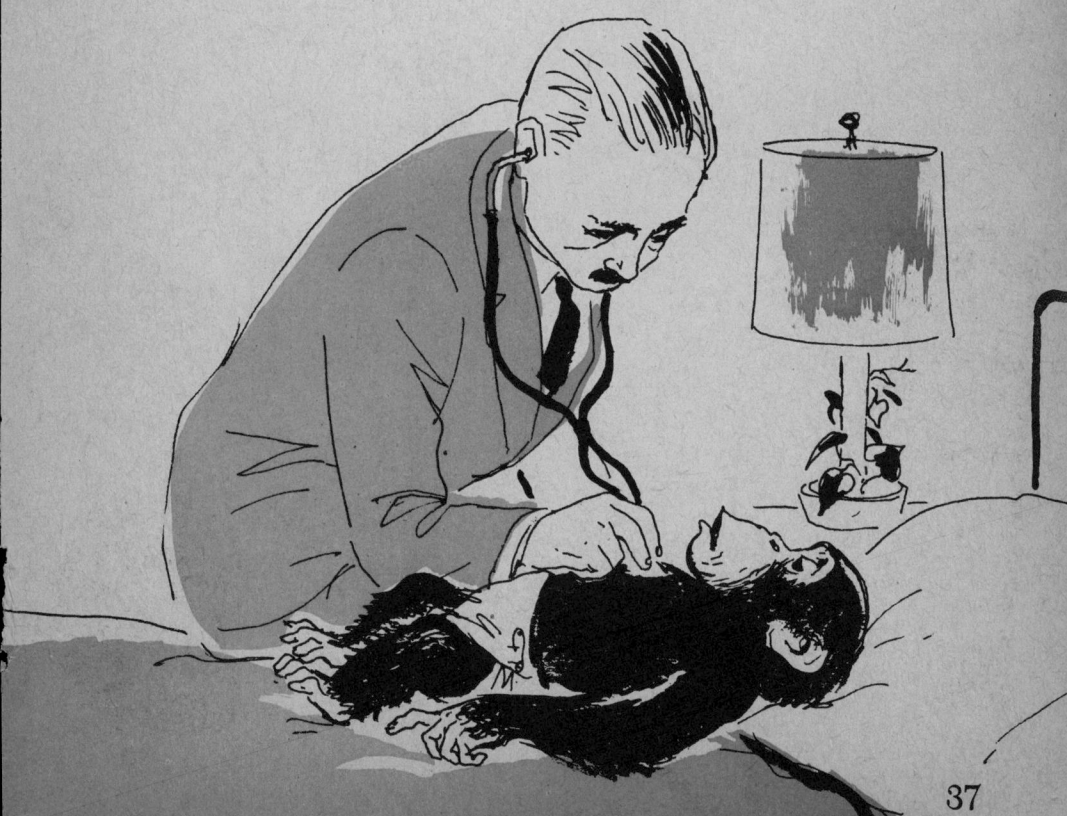

bronchitis. And pneumonia might set in."

He pulled out a needle and filled it with penicillin. "But this wonder drug may prevent it," he said.

Maggie cried with fright when she saw the needle, but Mr. Davis held her firmly while the doctor gave her the injection.

Then Dr. Sampson wrote something down on a slip of paper. "This is a prescription for another wonder drug," he said. "Give Maggie one pill after every meal and one before she goes to sleep. I hope they work."

For the next few days, Maggie was a very sick little chimp. She had one long coughing fit after the other.

Dr. Sampson warned the children to keep out of her room. "Each time Maggie coughs, she sprays the air with germs," he said. "Besides, Maggie must keep quiet. She is very, very sick."

"Will she die?" asked Peg.

"I hope not," replied the doctor.

Since Mr. Davis had to go to his pet store every day, Mother became Maggie's nurse. At first she complained about her job. But Peg and Tom helped out by doing most of the housework, and as Mother sat with the sick little chimp, she began to feel

sorry for her. Soon she was just as worried about Maggie as the rest of the family.

After four bad days, the coughing eased up, but it did not stop. Then Maggie's nose started running, and she sneezed quite often.

Dr. Sampson gave her more pills and said, "She has a head cold now. Try to teach her to blow her nose. Use paper handkerchiefs and throw them away. The handkerchiefs will be full of germs."

Teaching Maggie to blow her nose wasn't easy. Mrs. Davis tried to blow her own nose to show Maggie what to do. But the trouble was that Mrs. Davis didn't have a cold and she couldn't make her nose work right.

After a while, Maggie caught on and she managed some good hard blows.

The next thing was to get her to use a paper handkerchief. Maggie liked the handkerchiefs — that is, she liked to tear them up. It took some time to get her into the habit of wiping her nose.

Dr. Sampson became so interested in Maggie that he stopped in to visit her whenever he was in the neighborhood. After he saw that Maggie was careful about wiping her nose and coughing into a paper handkerchief, Dr. Sampson decided that it was safe for the children to play with her.

Maggie soon became very fond of Tom and Peg. There were many times when she tried to hug and kiss them. But they had to teach her not to do this as long as she still had her cold.

Although Maggie loved the children, she was jealous of them, too. If Tom and Peg played together and did not let her in on the game, she felt hurt. She often forced her way into the middle of what they were doing to make them let her play, too.

Peg and Tom managed to train Maggie very nicely. She learned how to go to the bathroom by herself and to wash her hands and face. Sometimes Tom forgot to brush his teeth after breakfast, but Maggie never did. She always went to the sink and took down her own toothbrush. Then Tom would follow and brush his teeth, too.

Maggie now drank out of a cup and used a spoon and fork. She ate a lot and she grew and grew. But she still coughed every once in a while.

As Maggie grew bigger, it became harder and harder to take care of her inside the house. The children went out to play whenever the weather was nice but Mr. Davis didn't dare let Maggie go outside. Yet she needed more room to run around in.

Maggie, in her way, did the best she could. She used the floor lamps as trees and climbed up on them. She loved to pull on the cords of the window blinds and open closet doors and swing on them.

Dr. Sampson said, "Well, growing children need plenty of exercise. So do growing apes. She needs to get out in the sunshine, too. The weather is getting warmer now, and I think, if you take Maggie out, she will soon get rid of her cough."

Looking at the children, Dr. Sampson added, "They need sunshine, too."

"Oh, they get plenty," said Father.

The weather forecast for the next day was warm and sunny. So Father said, "Let's go on a picnic. If we leave early in the morning, the neighbors won't see us. And we can go to Orange Lake where no one knows us."

By seven o'clock the next morning, the Davis family were on their way. Maggie was wearing her warm blue sailor suit and sitting up front between Mother and Father.

Suddenly Tom cried, "A police car is chasing after us!"

Father drew up to the side of the road and stopped.

A policeman stepped out of his car. He didn't

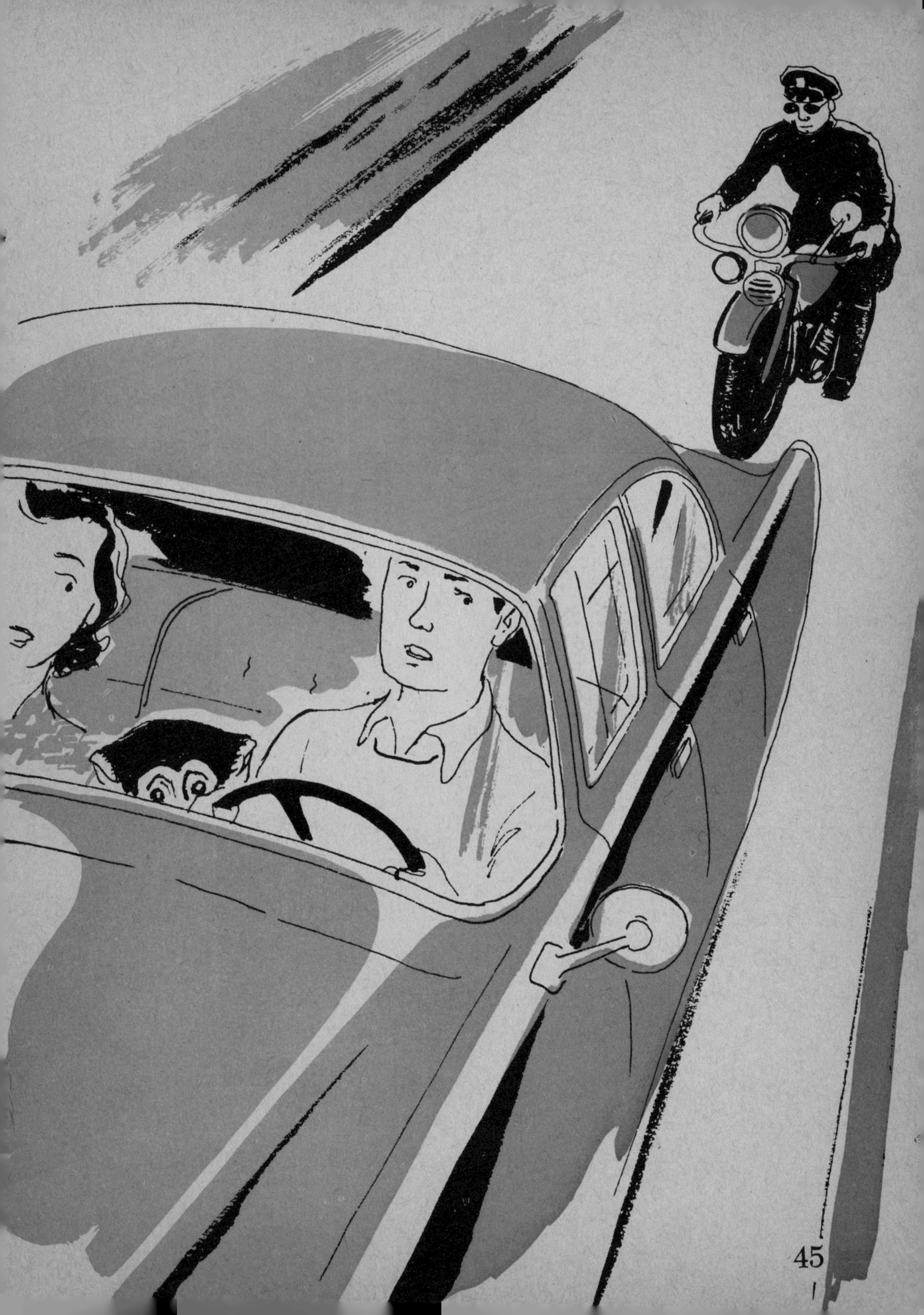

see Maggie and he began to talk to Mr. Davis in a gruff voice.

Maggie didn't like this one bit. Her hair began to stand on end and, without warning, she let out a loud bark. The policeman was so surprised that he almost fell over.

Maggie barked again and again.

The policeman laughed. "Golly, that certainly is a new kind of pet. She sure doesn't like me. Tell her that I just wanted to warn you to slow down. The road ahead is torn up. No hard feelings, eh, little chimp?" Then he held out his hand to Maggie.

She looked at Father. He was smiling. So Maggie smiled, too, and shook hands with the policeman.

Father then drove on. He didn't stop until he came to Orange Lake.

The first thing that Tom did was to chain Maggie to a tree. She seemed happy there and so he started to build a fire.

Maggie had never seen a fire before and she became terrified. She started to growl and to tug at her chain. All of a sudden she broke loose. Lickety-split, off into the woods she ran.

47

"Maggie!" shouted Father. "Come back! Come back!"

Tom and Peg raced after her. So did Father. But Maggie was faster in the woods than they were, and they soon lost sight of her.

For a whole hour they hunted for Maggie. Mr. Davis became very worried, and Peg started to cry.

But Tom said, "Let's call the police and ask them to send out a searching party."

"No, I don't want that. The story will be in all the papers," said Father.

Just then a big pine cone hit him on the head. As he looked up, a second cone hit him. "What in blazes——" he muttered. But before he could say anything else, a shower of cones rained down on him.

"Maggie!" yelled Tom. "Come down this minute!"

Maggie answered with another shower of cones.

"We'll have to think of some way of coaxing her down," said Father.

Peg beamed. "I have an idea. You know how

jealous Maggie is. Let's you and I hug and kiss each other."

When Maggie saw Peg throw her arms around her Father, she barked, "Uh-uh-uh!"

A pair of long, furry arms reached from branch to branch. Maggie swung over to the huggers. Suddenly she jumped down, right beside them. She lowered her head and fiercely tried to push her way between them.

Father laughed. "Why, Maggie! I didn't know you cared that much."

When they came back to the lake, Mrs. Davis hugged Maggie. "You impy chimp, don't you ever do that again."

Maggie returned the hug with a kiss.

The rest of the day went smoothly. Maggie ate wieners with the children and went for a boat ride.

Late in the afternoon, the Davis family left the lake. By then Maggie was so tired that she slept all the way home.

It was dark, and no one saw Mr. Davis carry Maggie back into the apartment house. "We'll have to do this again sometime," he said.

The next day Maggie was restless inside the house. Peg and Tom were baby-sitting with her, but she refused to mind them. When the doorbell

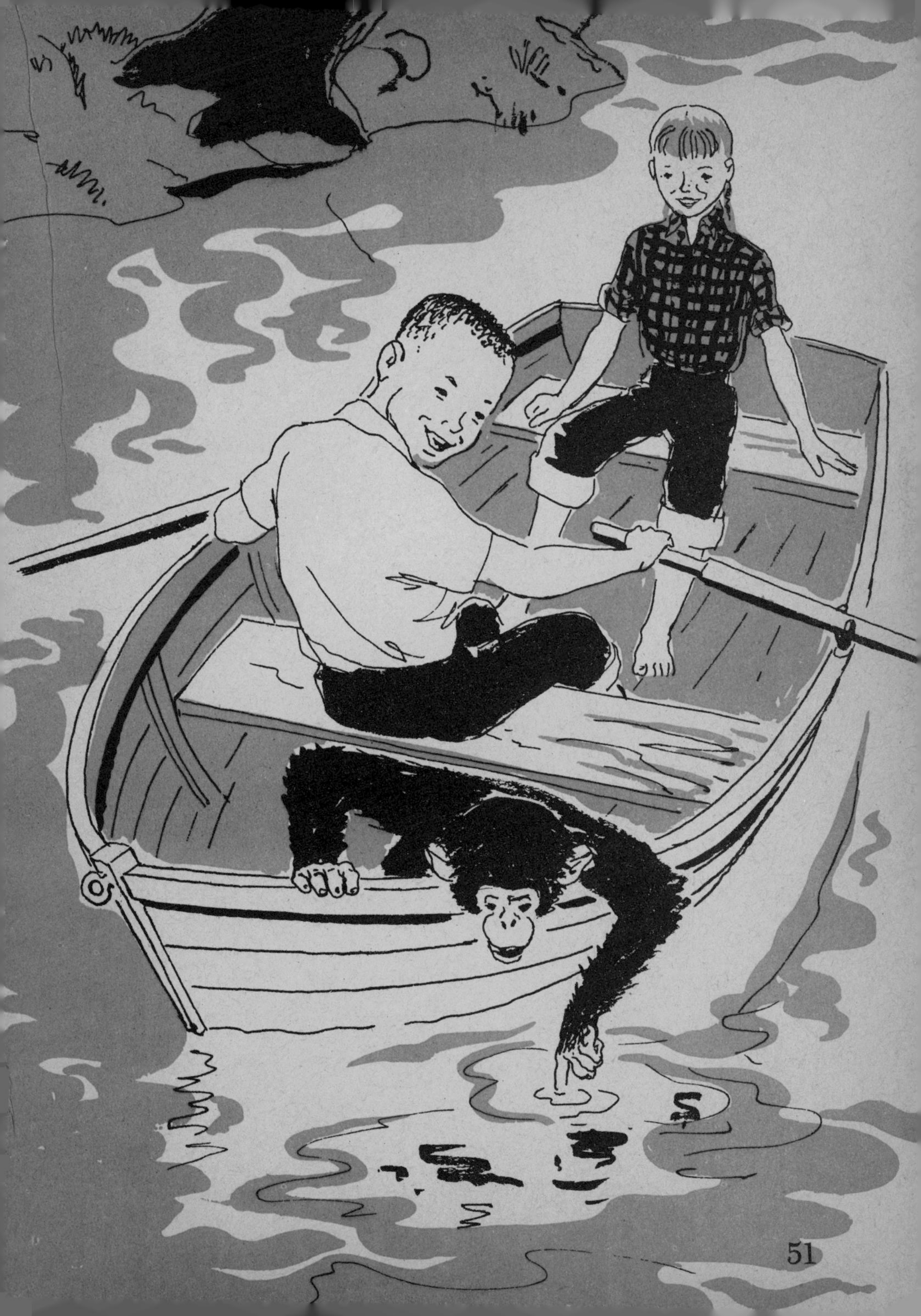

rang, Maggie ran down the hall.

Tom yelled, "Come back!"

Before he could grab her, Maggie had the door wide open. And there stood the lady who lived upstairs. In her arms was a package that had been left for the Davis family while they were out on their picnic.

When she saw Maggie, she forgot about the package and shrieked, "Help! Help!"

All the doors to the other apartments were flung open and dozens of people filled the outside hall. Maggie bared her teeth at them and started to bark.

"There's a mad ape in the house!" screamed the lady from downstairs. "Help! Help!"

Out dashed Mrs. Davis. "Listen!" she cried. "Maggie is just a pet. She won't hurt anyone."

After the excitement had quieted down, the phone rang. It was the police. They warned Mrs. Davis that if Maggie ever disturbed the peace again, she could not stay in the apartment.

Then one newspaper after another telephoned, wanting to take Maggie's picture. Each time Mrs. Davis said, "No."

Finally Mother said, "Let's get out of here."

Peg put on a big-brimmed doll's bonnet on Maggie and strapped her into the doll carriage.

Out on the street, no one noticed that there was a chimp in the carriage. So Mother said, "I guess we can go to the park."

The children headed straight for the zoo. Everything went fine until they got inside. And then there was an outburst. Every last monkey shrieked greetings to Maggie. And so did Alexander, the chimpanzee. He jumped on his swing and sailed through the air, screaming with delight.

Maggie broke out of her strap and scrambled over to Alexander's cage. He jumped down and ran to the bars. Then he reached out to pet her.

Maggie began to test one bar after another.

"Why, she's trying to get into that cage!" cried Peg.

"That's where she belongs," said a stern voice.

The children turned around and there stood the zoo keeper. "Where did you get that ape?" he demanded.

"Why, she's ours," said Mrs. Davis.

"Tell that to the park director—and to the police."

It was easy enough to explain to the park director who Maggie was. He said, "I wish we had her here in the zoo. Every child in the city would love her."

All the way home Peg kept saying, "I hope the zoo doesn't buy her. Oh, Mother, I promise you I won't let Maggie get us into any trouble. Please let's keep her."

"Please," begged Tom.

But when Father heard about what had happened in the park, he said, "Well, you know Maggie is really too big now for this little apartment. And she's over her cold. I really hope the zoo will buy her."

As the days went by, Maggie grew more and

more restless. Tom and Peg didn't sit with her very much now because Maggie was often too hard to manage.

One afternoon when Mother had a club meeting in the living room she asked Tom and Peg to keep Maggie out of mischief.

At first everything went along smoothly. Maggie played quietly, and so Tom decided to go into his room to read. Peg began to paint a picture.

Meanwhile Maggie sneaked out of the bedroom. She went straight into the kitchen. There she swung back and forth on the door of the kitchen cupboard. Then she spied an open jar of jam. She sat down and ate all the jam.

58

When she was finished, she went down the hall into Father's and Mother's room. She opened the closet door and spotted Mother's clothes. She pulled them out and began to dress herself up.

By the time the meeting was over, Maggie was wearing Mother's new spring hat and the skirt of her new suit. Jam stains were all over the skirt and the woodwork of the closet, too.

As Maggie heard footsteps come toward the bedroom, she quickly reached for a light bulb screwed into a wall socket. The bulb didn't come out and so she tore the entire fixture from the wall.

"Maggie!" screamed Mrs. Davis.

Both Tom and Peg jumped up and ran to see what had happened.

Maggie had never looked so funny in all her life. But the children didn't laugh. They saw that the electric fixture had been ripped from the wall and that jam stains were over everything. They heard their mother say angrily, "Tom and Peg, this is all your fault! You promised to mind Maggie! Fortunately she didn't get a shock. Maggie could have killed herself and perhaps caused a bad short circuit. Maggie, you're a menace."

Mother advanced toward Maggie to pull off her hat. But Maggie, who still clutched the light bulb,

59

bared her teeth and looked as if she were going to throw it at Mother.

Just then Father walked in. Maggie quieted down instantly and ran up to him as if he were her only friend.

When Father saw her jam-covered hands, he marched Maggie to the bathroom and made her wash herself.

"Spank her, too!" called Mother.

"No," said Father. "This will never happen again, because the zoo has bought Maggie."

Peg began to cry, even though she really knew that Maggie was too big and strong to be kept in a city apartment.

That night when Maggie was in her crib, Peg saw her hug the little chimp doll. Then she remembered how Maggie had tried to get into the cage in the zoo. She whispered, "You really do need a chimpanzee friend—someone as strong as you—for a playmate." Then she tiptoed out of the room.

The next day the Davis family took Maggie to the zoo. The minute the keeper opened the cage, Maggie ran right in.

Alexander hugged her, and soon she was riding on the swing with him.

Tom felt a lump in his throat, but he managed to say, "Good-by, Maggie."

Peg waved to her, but Maggie didn't wave back. She was too busy playing with Alexander.

"She's excited just now," said the zoo keeper. "Give her time to calm down. Then come back and see her as often as you wish. She'll always remember you."

"And we'll always remember Maggie," said Peg.